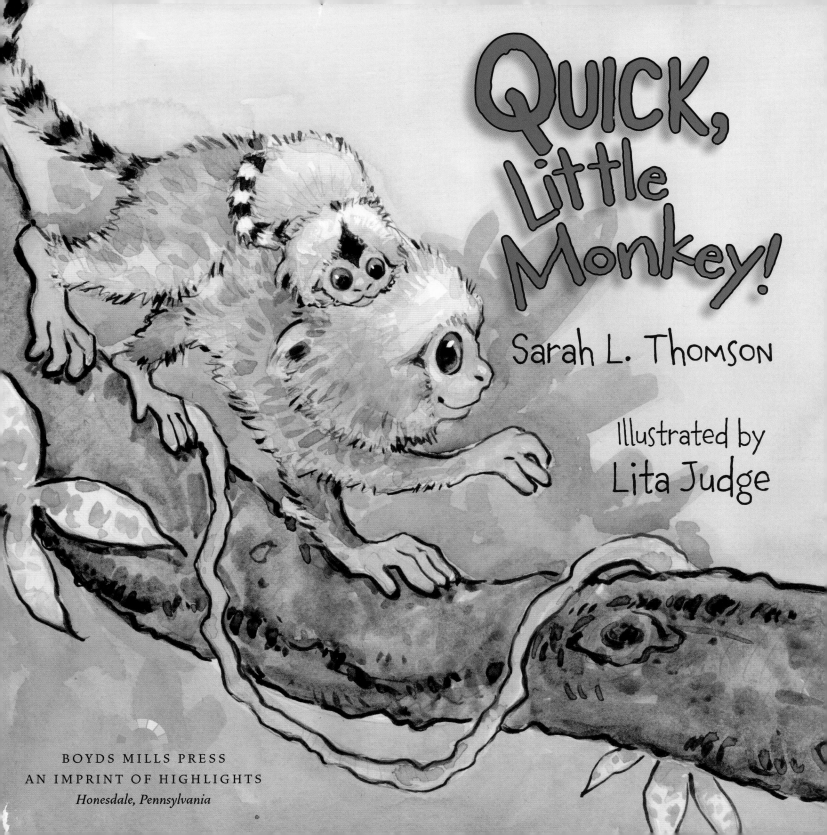

QUICK, Little Monkey!

Sarah L. Thomson

Illustrated by
Lita Judge

BOYDS MILLS PRESS
AN IMPRINT OF HIGHLIGHTS
Honesdale, Pennsylvania

Little Monkey loved to fly.

She swept from vine to vine. She skimmed from branch to branch.

"Hold tight,"
said Papa Monkey.

Little Monkey did.
Fingers in fur,
arms clinging,
tail swinging,

Little Monkey flew with Papa
high and safe and quick
in the bright, loud, green world.

Far above,
wings cast a shadow.
"Hide here,"
said Papa.

Little Monkey did.

Far below,
soft footsteps padded.
"Keep still,"
said Papa.

Little Monkey did.

A blue and busy beetle
buzzed past her nose.
A black and shiny ant
tickled her toes.

But Little Monkey didn't move
from her small safe space.

A flower spread bright wings to float away.

Little Monkey squealed with glee.

She snatched and slipped . . .

. . . and
tumbled
and fell
out of
the world . . .

. . . down into a quiet dark

of slow roots

and still earth

and cold shadow.

She found
a small safe space.
Hide here,
thought Little Monkey.

She saw
a flash of fur.
Keep still,
thought Little Monkey.

She smelled
hot, hungry breath.

She touched a slim, smooth vine.
Hold tight!
thought Little Monkey.

Strong legs leaped.

Sharp claws slashed.

But Little Monkey was too fast.

She **clung** and

climbed from vine to vine . . .

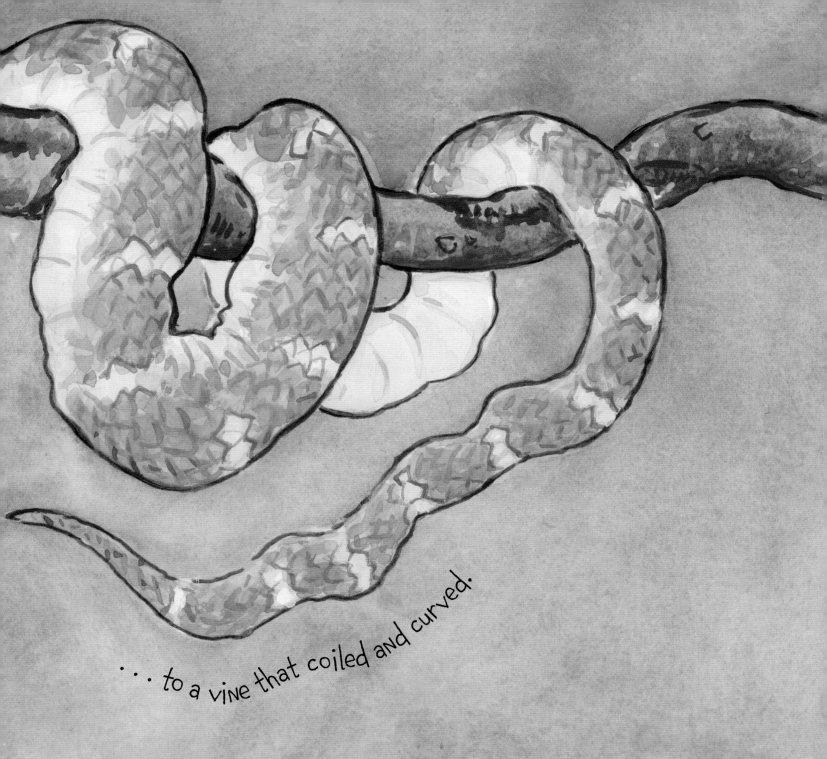

. . . to a vine that coiled and curved.

It opened
two eager eyes.

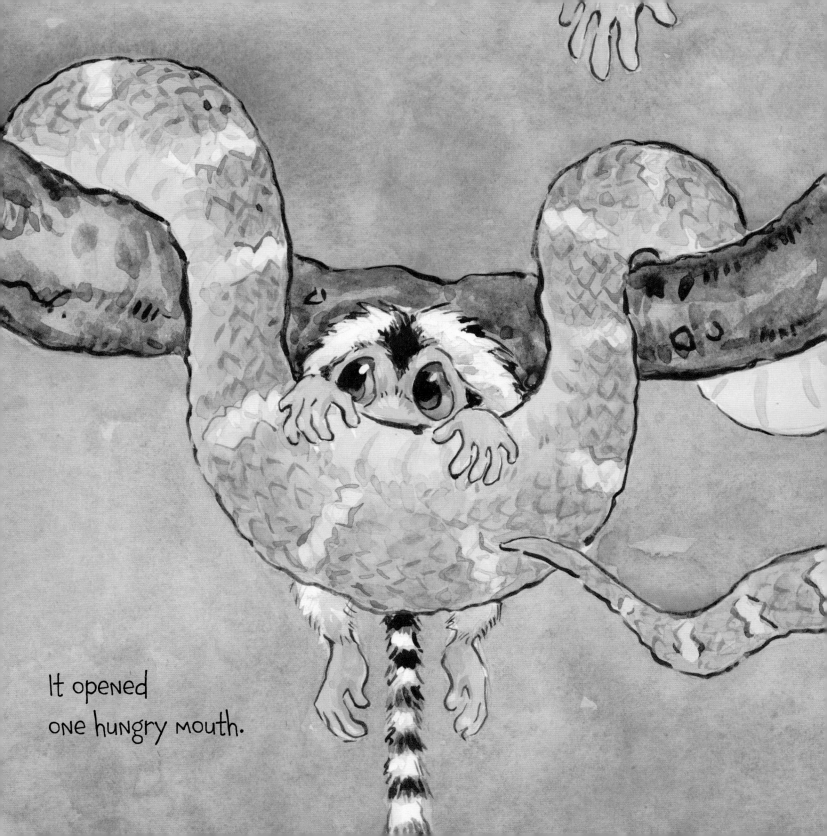

It opened
one hungry mouth.

Quick, Little Monkey!

Fly, Little Monkey!

And Little Monkey flew.

"Hold tight,"
said Papa Monkey.
Little Monkey did.

Little Monkey and Papa
soared and swooped
high into the safe and bright,
loud and leafy
world.

Author's Note

Little Monkey and her father are pygmy marmosets, the world's smallest monkey. An adult weighs about as much as a stick of butter, and a baby could easily curl up in your hand. They live in the forests of South America, and spend most of their time high in the branches.

Pygmy marmosets gather in small groups, called troops, and fathers do much of the childcare. They carry the youngest babies piggyback and bring them to their mothers to be nursed.

These tiny monkeys are hunted by a number of predators. In this story, Little Monkey must escape from a black hawk-eagle, an ocelot, and a young emerald tree boa. Luckily her Papa looks out for her and teaches her to look out for herself!

For my dad—of course
—SLT

For Rod Judge
—LJ

Text copyright © 2016 by Sarah L. Thomson
Illustrations copyright © 2016 by Lita Judge
All rights reserved.
For information about permission to reproduce selections from this book, contact permissions@highlights.com.

Boyds Mills Press
An Imprint of Highlights
815 Church Street
Honesdale, Pennsylvania 18431
Printed in China
ISBN: 978-1-62979-100-5
Library of Congress Control Number: 2015946897

First edition
The text of this book is set in Chauncy Decaf.
The illustrations are done in graphite pencil and watercolor.
10 9 8 7 6 5 4 3 2 1